LIVE
YOUTH FICTION

Dear Kate

Marian Iseard

Published in association with
The Basic Skills Agency

Hodder & Stoughton
A MEMBER OF THE HODDER HEADLINE GROUP

Acknowledgements
Cover: Darren Lock
Illustrations: Jim Eldridge

Orders; please contact Bookpoint Ltd, 39 Milton Park, Abingdon, Oxon OX14 4TD. Telephone: (44) 01235 400414, Fax: (44) 01235 400454. Lines are open from 9.00–6.00, Monday to Saturday, with a 24 hour message answering service. Email address: orders@bookpoint.co.uk

British Library Cataloguing in Publication Data
A catalogue record for this title is available from the British Library

ISBN 0 340 77612 9

First published 2000
Impression number 10 9 8 7 6 5 4 3 2 1
Year   2005 2004 2003 2002 2001 2000

Typeset by GreenGate Publishing Services, Tonbridge, Kent.
Printed in Great Britain for Hodder and Stoughton Educational, a division of Hodder Headline Plc, 338 Euston Road, London NW1 3BH, by Atheneum Press, Gateshead, Tyne & Wear

Dear Kate

Contents

1

February 3rd

Dear Kate

I hope you don't mind me writing to you
I mean, me being a boy.
I've seen your problem page in my sister's
magazine and I thought you might be able
to help me.
I don't know who else to ask.

The thing is, my problem isn't just mine.
It's Sarah's too, my girlfriend.
And it's the worst kind,
the sort that can't be undone.
I suppose you can guess what it is,
so I may as well tell you now –
Sarah is pregnant.

I know what you'll think
but we had been careful.
We know about contraception and all that.
It gets drummed into you at school
until you can't not know.
But just this once we took a risk.
We thought it would be all right – just once.
But it wasn't. It isn't.
Now it feels like nothing will ever
be all right again.

I know you can't wave a magic wand.
No one can. But I thought you might tell me
where I can go for some advice.
Without anyone having to know –
I mean parents. (We haven't told them yet,
we can't face it.)
I just need to talk to someone.
Someone who can help.

Sarah doesn't know I've written to you.
She won't talk to anyone, she says.
I think she's just hoping it'll go away.
If only …

Can you write to me at my house?
I've put an envelope in with my address on,
like it says on your problem page.
Please write soon, if you can.

Yours truly,

Lee

Lee

2

February 20th

Dear Kate

Thanks for your letter,
and for the leaflets you sent.
I had to make sure I got to the post first –
so my Mum didn't see the letter.
Not that she'd open it.
But she'd ask what was in it.
You know what they're like.

I read the leaflet about the
family planning clinic.
I asked Sarah if she'd go.
Just to talk to someone, get some advice.
I told her that no one will say anything
to our parents. But she won't.

'Somebody might see me going in
and tell my Mum,' she said.

I said she could wear dark glasses and
a false moustache, but she didn't think
that was very funny.

Anyway, I'm a bit worried about Sarah.
She seems to be changing her mind about things.
I suppose I'd thought that she felt
the same as me.
That we'd made a big mistake and that
we had to sort it out.
You know what I mean. Abortion.
Well the other day Sarah said that
she didn't think she could do that.
I nearly died. What else can we do?

Look – I'm 17, Sarah's 16.
We're too young, don't you think?
We can't have a baby, not now.
She's got her GCSEs coming up
and I'm at college.
I'm doing an engineering course.
Next year I'll be looking for a job.

I'm only thinking of what's best.
What about money?
What about all the things we want to do?
I mean, I don't want to be a millionaire.
I just want to be able to go out
with my friends. Maybe buy a car
and some decent clothes, CDs – all that.

I think Sarah agrees with me really,
but we can't hang around.
We need to get this sorted
before it's too late.

Sometimes it feels like everything's too late.
I feel like rushing round to friends to warn them.
To say, 'be careful – don't do what we did,
don't get caught'.
But why should they listen? We didn't.

What shall I do Kate?

Yours miserably,

Lee

3

March 3rd

Dear Kate

Thanks for writing again.
Yes, I know what you mean.
About giving Sarah time to decide.
About trying to agree things together.
I just wish she'd talk to someone else as well.
Someone who would say the same as me –
that we're too young to have kids.

You said it can be very difficult for someone to
get over having an abortion.
That Sarah might regret it.
Well I think she'd regret being tied down
by a baby even more.
Never having any money.
Never being able to go out.
I don't think she'd be happy.

Yesterday we had a big row.
I thought that was it – the end.
Sarah said she didn't want to see me again
and walked off.
She only got as far as the park gates mind you,
so she can't have really meant it.

I'll tell you what happened.
We'd gone for a walk with my dog, Scruff.
I decided to say what was on my mind.
I told Sarah that if we waited too long
it might be too late.
I said, 'Why don't you go and talk
to the school nurse?'

She went really quiet. Then suddenly
she turned and started shouting at me.
Awful things about killing babies,
and not really loving her.

In the end I started yelling back.
I couldn't help it, I was getting so mad.
That was when Sarah stormed off,
telling me to get lost.
When she got to the gates she changed her mind.
She came back for another go,
started all over again.

I don't know what would have happened
if it hadn't been for Scruff.
He came and sat between us and howled,
really loud. It was as if he was saying,
'Shut up you two!'

We both laughed, and then Sarah cried.
Then (I wouldn't tell anyone else this) so did I.
It was just like when we went to see *Titanic*.

Well we made it up,
but we haven't agreed anything.
We just didn't talk about it after that.
Not until we got back to Sarah's house.
I was just leaving and she said,
'We could get a flat.
Your parents might be able to help.'

Just because my Dad's got a good job,
she thinks they're rolling in it. Huh.

The thing is, Kate,
I think she's living in fantasy land.
I don't think she knows how much
a baby costs. Well, neither do I
but I can guess. Too much.

Sarah says I'm only thinking about myself,
but I'm not. I'm thinking of everyone.
Is it fair to bring a baby into the world
if you can't look after it properly?
What do you think Kate?

Yours worriedly,

Lee

Lee

4

March 14th

Dear Kate

This won't be a very long letter.
I've just got a few minutes
before I go into college.
I'm sitting on a bench outside,
watching everyone else go in.
They all look so carefree.
I think I should be like them,
I used to be like them.

Now all the time I've got this worry
at the back of my mind.
Well, more like the front of my mind really.
I can't think about anything else.
I can't work.

I wish I could go back in time,
but I can't. That's the worst thing, Kate.
There's just no undoing what's done.

I know we should tell someone now.
But if Sarah and I can't agree,
what chance will we have
when everyone's sticking their nose in?
They'll all try to tell us what to do.
I don't think I can stand that.

Sarah won't be able to hide it much longer.
She's been feeling a bit sick in the mornings,
not wanting her breakfast.
She told her Mum she's on a diet.
She reckons her Mum's been giving her
funny looks, as though she suspects something.

Anyway, I've been feeling a bit helpless.
Since we had that big row in the park
I don't dare talk about you-know-what.
See, I can't even write the word.
Yesterday I met Sarah out of school
and we walked home together.

She asked me what I was thinking about.
I said, 'I was wondering if my Saturday job
would pay me in nappies instead of money.'

I was trying to make her laugh
(she hasn't smiled for days)
but she didn't seem to see the joke.
She squeezed my arm.

'I'm glad you're thinking about practical things
like nappies,' she said.
What can I do Kate?
It seems she's made her mind up.

I've got to go now.

Yours helplessly,

Lee

Lee

5

March 26th

Dear Kate

Thanks for your letter.
Yes, I can see that for Sarah
it must be different. More difficult.
Her body's going through lots of changes.
But she could try seeing it from my
point of view as well.
After all, don't men have rights?

I just think we're too young.
We've made a mistake – but do we
have to pay for it for the rest of our lives?
Can't we have the chance to start again?

Anyway, listen to this.
My cousin Kevin came round.
He's married to Sally.
They have a new baby, Natalie.
Mum told me to make sure I was home.

'I'm sure Kevin would like to see you,' she said.

Can you believe it? It was just what I needed.

When they arrived Natalie was asleep
in her car seat.
She looked like a little monkey.
Her face was all screwed up.
When she woke up
the first thing she did was poo herself.
What a smell! Sally took her off
to get cleaned up.

Kevin said, 'Isn't she great?
I never thought I'd like babies –
but she's special.'

Well, I didn't say much,
just a few polite questions.
Like how many nappies does she get through.
I mean, I want to know these things.
My Mum gave me a look as if she thought
I'd gone off my head.
I suppose normally it's the last thing
I'd be thinking about – nappies.

Then Sally came down with Natalie
(smelling a bit nicer now).
She put her straight in my arms.
Without even asking!
Natalie started crying and everyone laughed,
like it was the funniest thing they'd ever seen.
And nobody came over to take her away.

Mum said, 'Bounce her up and down a bit.'

They were all talking about
Kevin and Sally's new house.

I got up and walked her round the house.
She was still crying
so I started trying to make her laugh.
Pulling funny faces and making silly noises.
The sort of thing you tell yourself you'll never,
ever be seen doing.
Then suddenly she started laughing.
Really, laughing – this little gurgling noise.
Then I laughed, and she laughed some more.

By now Kevin had come to help me out.
He said, 'She must like you.
She doesn't do that for everyone.'
Do you know what Kate?
I felt sort of proud, that I'd stopped her crying.
Don't get me wrong.
That was just one hour of babyness.
It doesn't mean I want it full-time.
At least, not right now.

Yours confusingly

Lee

6

April 6th

Dear Kate

It's very late, but I can't sleep.
Everything's gone crazy here.
You know what you said, that I should tell my
parents?
Well today I did. Had to really.
Don't worry, I'm still alive – just.

The thing is, Sarah's Mum worked it out.
Mums can tell these things can't they?

So this morning she got Sarah on her own.
She made her admit it,
got the whole story from her.
Later on Sarah phoned me. She was crying.
She said she was crying because her Mum
had been so great.
She hadn't gone mad or anything.
Sarah said if she'd known she'd be so good
about it she'd have told her ages ago.

Then she said, 'You'd better tell your parents
because once my Dad knows
he'll be straight over.'

'Great,' I said. 'Your Dad's never liked me.'

'Yes he does,' she said.

'Well he soon won't.'

I don't know which I dreaded most –
my parents or Sarah's dad.

Anyway, there was no more putting it off.

It's funny isn't it, how sometimes it's worse
when someone doesn't say anything?
When they just go quiet?
I said, 'Sarah's going to have a baby.'

There was this long silence.
All the times I've wished my parents would stop
going on at me – today I wanted them
to say something, anything.
Mum's face sort of crumpled up.
I knew she wanted to cry but she didn't.
Finally she just said, 'What will you do?'
As if I know. Dad was all thin-lipped.
He kept saying, 'I can't believe it',
and 'how could you be so stupid?'

The next thing, Sarah's parents were
on the phone, saying they were coming round.

You could see her Dad was furious.
As soon as he came in he said,
'You've got a lot to answer for young man.'

Sarah's Mum was trying to calm him down.
She said, 'It takes two you know.'

Dad gave him a beer,
then they all sat down round the table.
They started talking about us
as if we were invisible.
As if we didn't have any say.
They all seemed to be saying the same thing.
That Sarah couldn't possibly have the baby.
That we're too young.

It was strange Kate,
hearing someone else say that.
Strange because they made it sound
as if it was up to them.
I kept thinking – what do I really want?
What will happen to me and Sarah
if she has an abortion?
She might end up hating me.

I wish I knew what to do Kate.

Yours unhappily

Lee

7

April 7th

Dear Kate

I know you haven't had time to answer
the last letter but everything is happening so fast.

Somehow writing it down makes me feel better.
It gets things clearer in my head.
I hope you don't mind me taking up so much time.

It's the day after yesterday.
I mean, the day after I told my parents.

This morning Sarah phoned.
'Let's go for a walk,' she said.
'We must talk – on our own.'
'OK,' I said.

We didn't argue this time.
I told Sarah how scared I was at the idea of
being a father. She told me that she was scared
of how she'd feel if she had an abortion.

'I know that's what Mum and Dad think is best.
But I might hate myself, afterwards,' she said.

I said, 'You might hate me too.'

She thought for a minute.
'Maybe I would.'

Well that was honest.

Then she said, 'But I don't want you to
end up hating me. If I have the baby
I won't ask you to live with us.'

That was even more honest.

I felt like I was being counted out of things.
First the parents going on about how Sarah was too young to be a mother.
They hadn't even asked me what I thought.
Now Sarah was saying that if she had the baby she'd do it all on her own. Without me.

'What if I wanted to live with you?' I said.

She didn't answer.
I suppose I haven't shown much sign of wanting to play happy families up to now, have I?

When we went home we still hadn't made a decision, but at least we'd listened to each other.

Yours undecidedly

Lee

Lee

8

May 20th

Dear Kate

I'm sorry there's been such a long gap.
You must wonder what's happened.
Well – quite a lot.

Soon after our parents found out
I met some friends for a coffee.
They were all talking about the usual things –
music, girls, who fancies who.

I sat there thinking that this used to be my life.
I had nothing more to worry about
than where to go that night.
It could be like that again
if Sarah didn't have the baby.

Then I thought, no.
My life will never be that simple again.
Everything has changed.
If Sarah gets rid of the baby
she won't want me around anymore.
I'd just remind her of what she'd done.

I stood up.
'I've got to go,' I said.
Everyone looked at me as if I'd gone mad.
I ran all the way to Sarah's house.
I just hoped she'd be in.
Lucky for me she was.
She came to the door and stared at the state
of me – dripping with sweat.

'What's the matter?' she asked.

'You've got to do what's right for you,' I said.
'It's got to be your decision,
but whatever it is I want us to still be together.'

She smiled.
'I know,' she said. 'And I have decided.'

That was six weeks ago.
Now Sarah's getting bigger all the time.
She's not going to school any more.
She has a home tutor instead.

Everyone is slowly getting used to the idea.
Sarah's Dad calmed down once he got over
the shock of being a grandad. My Mum's
started knitting. Dad even joked that
he'd taken out a season ticket for Mothercare!

We've worked out what we're going to do.
Sarah will have a year off studying
to look after the baby.
Maybe she'll go to college next year.
She's going to live at home for a while.
I'll be able to see her and the baby
in the evenings.

When I finish my course
I'll be looking for a job.
We're going to put our names down then
for a council flat. Well, that's the plan.
I know things won't be easy.
In fact it'll be hard work
and not much time to ourselves.

We're making the best of things
but I still think – if only we'd been careful.
If only this … if only that …
I know there'll be lots of times
when I just want to be one of the lads.
Times when I'll wish I'd been sensible
and not got myself into this.

Last week a social worker rang to ask Sarah
if she'd take part in a new project.
It would mean going into schools
with the baby. Talking to the school-kids
and telling them her story.
She said yes, and would I come too.
I think I'd like to.

Because then maybe they might think –
it *could* happen to me.

I don't suppose I'll write again.
Except to tell you when the baby's born!
Thanks for all your help Kate.

Yours gratefully

Lee